Walt Disney's
AMERICAN CLASSICS
Paul Bunyan

Starlight Editions

Twin Books

Early one morning after a ferocious storm, a huge cradle washed up near a town in Maine. Inside the cradle was the biggest baby anyone had ever seen. It took the milk of five cows to fill his bottle!

The townfolk adopted him and named him Paul Bunyan, because they thought he should have the kind of name that sounded like a big guy's name!

Paul grew into a good lad and everybody liked him. He went to school just like all the other kids, but he was too big to fit inside the classrooom. So he sat outside and handed his lessons to the teacher by lifting the roof.

When school let out, all the kids would head for the old swimming hole. For huge Paul it was more like a bathtub!

Paul was interested in a lot of things as a youngster, but as he got older and bigger, he spent more and more time in the woods watching the loggers cut trees.

The townfolk noticed Paul's fascination with logging, and on his sixteenth Christmas they gave him a present that was to change his life forever and turn him into a legend.

It was a great, big, beautiful axe—just the right size!

MERRY
Christmas
PAUL

12

With that big double-bladed axe, Paul could cut trees faster than most men cut weeds.

Wherever Paul logged he was followed by prospective farmers, for he could clear enough land for a whole farm *in one day*.

Paul logged so fast that soon most of the forests were cut, and people moved in and built towns using lumber made from the logs that Paul and his fellow loggers had cut.

Life in the East was getting too citified for a fellow like Paul, who was sixty-three axe handles tall, so one day he headed west, in search of more forests and new adventures.

Soon winter came, and during the first blizzard of the season it was so cold that the snow itself turned blue! It was during this storm that Paul came upon a young baby ox, frozen blue and shivering in the snow.

"Here, big guy," said Paul, picking him up under one arm and holding him close to try to thaw him out.

Even after he'd thawed out,
the big ox stayed blue.
    "You're such a cute fella," said Paul, "I
think I'll call you Babe—Babe the Blue Ox!"
    Babe grew fast, and overnight he was twice
as big as a barn. Paul thought it was great to
have a pal as big as he was. So did Babe!

Not only was Babe Paul's closest companion, but he was mighty strong, too.

When Paul set up his logging camp near a river that had too many bends in it to float logs, he tied a length of rope and an anchor to Babe's yoke, and Babe pulled that river straight as a pine log!

Paul and Babe kept moving westward. As they were passing through Minnesota, they got confused during a ferocious rainstorm. Completely lost, they wandered around in circles for days.

The big puddles left by their footprints remained full of water, and to this day people still call Minnesota "The Land of Ten Thousand Lakes."

By the end of the summer, Paul and Babe had reached Wyoming. They were so glad to finally be out West that they got into a friendly wrestling match, and they kicked up a whole mountain range, which is now called the Grand Tetons. After the match they were pretty dusty, so Paul found a big mountain stream which he used to make a shower bath for him and Babe. When they'd finished, they went off and left it running, and it's now called Yellowstone Falls.

Out West among the giant trees there were big logging camps that were just the kind of places for Paul.

Now the loggers were big eaters. The head cook, Sourdough Sam, and his crew of forty served up hotcakes stacked to the ceiling, mountains of ten pound steaks and biscuits by the cart-load.

But no one was a bigger eater than Paul Bunyan, so Sourdough Sam's men made special six-foot doughnuts for him—and, of course, for Babe, too.

Babe got special treatment from Ole Olson, the camp black-smith. The ox shoes he made for Babe were so heavy that when Ole lifted them, his feet sank deep in the ground.

One hot summer day, Paul brought a load of corn into camp, and the corn grew so hot in the scorching sun it began to pop.

"It's a blizzard!" cried the men, and they bundled up and shivered at the sight of it. A herd of cattle took one look at the blizzard and turned blue on the spot!

Late that fall the skeeter bees were flying North and South—they couldn't remember which direction to go, since they had a bee stinger on one end and a "skeeter" stinger on the other.

Their buzzing became louder and louder as a stranger came chugging into camp aboard a shiny new locomotive.

"My name," said the stranger, "is Joe Muffaw, and I'm gonna show you something you won't believe. I've got an automatic tree-cutting machine and a log-pulling locomotive that'll do your work in half the time."

Paul was angry. "Out *here* we use a double-bladed axe for cutting and oxen for pulling, Little Fella."

37

But Joe Muffaw continued to brag, so a contest was organized to see who could pull a triple load of logs faster—the locomotive, or Babe the Blue Ox.

"Come on, Babe!" cried the loggers, as he and the locomotive pulled with all their might, snorting and puffing.

When it was over…

... Babe lost by half an inch.

Sadly, Paul and Babe decided to say "So long" to their friends and head North.

Whatever happened to Paul Bunyan and Babe? Well, some folks say that logging machines put Paul out of business. Others say that Paul felt crowded, and went to Alaska, where the logging is endless and a man and his ox have plenty of room.

If you're sixty-three axe handles high like Paul, you need a lot of room!

This edition published by Starlight Editions,
an imprint of Dorset Press, a division of Marboro Books Corp.,
by arrangement with Twin Books

Produced by
Twin Books
15 Sherwood Place
Greenwich, CT 06830

ISBN 0-88029-360-8

Designed, edited and illustrated by
American Graphic Systems, San Francisco

Printed in Hong Kong in 1989